31 Days
Of Growth
And Reflection

Written by:
April Scales

Cadmus Publishing
www.cadmuspublishing.com

Take these next 31 days to journal on each daily meditation. Write your feelings and emotions. You'll be surprised at what may be revealed to you. Use this as a time to grow and reflect on areas that can be improved upon.

We cannot exist without each other. Our diversities are what make us unique. We are a small piece in the Creator's puzzle.

Day 1

Even those who seem to have it all together have room for improvement. I'm sure there are some areas in your life that you could be better. They won't get any better or be any different unless you make an effort to change. Change is scary but omnipotent. Try it.

* Meditate on three aspects of your life in which you want to grow.

Day 2

Apologizing is not easy for everyone, especially if you're one of those who are never wrong. Growing spiritually is about being humble enough to admit failure. Humble yourself to someone you've wronged and let go of what's holding you back.

* Write a letter of apology to someone even if you don't mail it.

Day 3

It's important to laugh at your own foibles. If you can't take a joke, you can't dish one. Besides, it takes fewer muscles to smile than to frown.

* Laugh at yourself.

Day 4

Embrace your inner child. We forget our innocence. Don't you miss skipping jumping rope, or perhaps Candy Land? Be a kid again just for today.

* Play a childhood game.

Day 5

So many times we go about our day without appreciating the sun that rose to greet us. Serotonin is so beneficial. It's nature's happy drug.

* Embrace the sun and notice how it feels against your skin.

✦ 18 ✦

Day 6

Do you remember a time when you were disobedient and had to sit in the corner for what seemed like an eternity? Now that you're an adult with responsibilities, what would you give for five minutes of QT?

* Sit for five minutes in complete silence.

Day 7

You may be the one who save's someone's life. Have you ever felt alone and as if no one cared? Nod your head and smile at someone you pass today. It may be just the life support that someone needs.

* Acknowledge a stranger today. Smile.

Day 8

Have you ever heard the expression, "It's better to give than to receive?" There's always someone less fortunate then yourself. Give a little and receive a lot.

* Contribute to someone in need.

Day 9

Oooh. A toughie. Who doesn't have a comfort food or drink? Caffeine? Sugar? Alcohol? Sacrifice it just for today. Fasting provides mental clarity.

*Detox your body for 24 hours and see what a difference a day makes.

Day 10

Let natural light in as much as possible. Rearrange your room or house (Feng Sheü). Allow the positive energy to flow. Make a simple change, like turning your shoes in the opposite direction.

* Rearranging your room may get your life in order.

40

Day 11

I'm a bit of a snob (I admit it). Sometimes we're too prideful to reach out. If no one ever goes first, we'll all be last.

* Contact someone whom you haven't heard from in a while.

Day 12

It's relaxing to receive a massage, but we don't always have the time or money. Give yourself a massage. You know what feels good to you. Treat yourself.

* Give yourself or someone a massage.

Day 13

There's nothing more unappealing than a lazy person. If the piece of paper that you dropped needs to go in the trash, put it there. Hold your head up when you walk. What you don't do is just as important as what you do.

* Be proactive!

Day 14

Do your best! Don't try to keep up with the Joneses! Forgive yourself when you fail. "To err is human, to forgive is divine."

* Forgive.

Day 15

Listen to yourself breathe. Is it erratic? Steady? Reflect on a situation that you could've avoided if only you would have paused and took a deep breath.

* Just breathe.

Day 16

No matter how old we get, we're never too old to learn. Knowledge is power. Never relinquish your power.

* Pick a word out of the dictionary, learn it, use it, and add it to your vocabulary.

64

Day 17

Flowers are beautiful, aren't they? How often do we take the time to pause and admire their beauty? What is no one ever paused to admire our beauty?

* Stop the smell the roses (flowers), literally.

68

Day 18

Puzzles have been known to reduce your risk of Alzheimer's. That's a pretty simple task. Strengthen your memory, you may need/want to reflect on the past one day.

* Do a crossword or puzzle today.

Day 19

I would probably run out of room if I named all of the things that I was grateful for. I hope your list is lengthy also.

* Name something small that you're grateful for (ex: you can brush your teeth, tie your shoes, or walk).

Day 20

I don't mean a computer screen, tablet, or subtitle on a TV. I want you to be pre-historic, Don't forget what existed first. It laid the foundation for what we have today.

* Read a newspaper, book, or periodical.

+ 80 +

Day 21

How many of us hold onto clothes that no longer fit, papers that need to be discarded, or just plain old junk? It takes up space. The same way we physically hold onto clutter, you hold onto it emotionally as well.

* Discard your clutter. Let your JUNK go!

Day 22

In my mind I can sing. I don't think my neighbors agree, but nothing brings a bigger smile to my heart than to have "my jam" come on the radio. I'm totally in character then.

* Belt out your favorite song and be in the moment.

Day 23

Life can throw you a curve ball when you least expect it. You're perfectly fine one minute and at death's door the next. You may be just what the doctor ordered to make someone feel better.

* Do something of value for someone under-the-weather.

Day 24

Amongst our busy days, sleep is necessary. How many of us get the proper amount? Sleep is when your body repairs itself. Don't you deserve healing?

* Get seven hours of sleep.

Day 25

Fast food can turn into fat food. Try to get a nutritionally balanced meal. You get out of your body exactly what you put in.

* Make food your frenemy. If you put the good in, It's your friend. If you put the bad in, it'll be your enemy. Yeah, it's really that simple.

Day 26

Isn't it relaxing to take a nice, long shower or bubble bath? It seems like all of my cares wash away.

* Wash all of your negativity down the drain today.

Day 27

People watch you more than you realize. You'd be surprised at who may emulate your every move, or at least the ones they see.

* Be a teacher! You are being watched even when you are not watching.

Day 28

Without mistakes, there would be no growth. We must get knocked down in order to get back up.

* Applaud your failures; they've made you a better version of yourself.

Day 29

No one is right 100% of the time. How boring would the world be if everyone was perfect? There's only One and we don't want His job.

* Admit when you're wrong and move on.

Day 30

You owe yourself a little exercise. It'll help you as you age. It makes you look and feel better and it's a great way to relieve stress. Get moving!

* Get 30 minutes of exercise today.

Day 31

Whatever you answer to will be a part of your legacy. Treat people as you want to be treated.

* If you answer to B*@!#, that's how you will be remembered.

www.ingramcontent.com/pod-product-compliance
Lightning Source LLC
Chambersburg PA
CBHW060556100726

47907CB00005B/1382